GW00854877

Especially for

_____

THE
NIGHT
BEFORE
CHRISTMAS

THE NIGHT BEFORE CHRISTMAS

A Visit from St. Nicholas

by CLEMENT C. MOORE

Illustrated by REGINALD BIRCH

HARCOURT, INC.

Orlando • Austin • New York • San Diego
Toronto • London

Manufactured in China

Twas the night before Christmas,
  when all through the house
Not a creature was stirring,
  not even a mouse;

The stockings were hung
    by the chimney with care,
In hopes that St. Nicholas
    soon would be there;

The children were nestled
all snug in their beds,
While visions of sugar-plums
danced in their heads;

And Mamma in her 'kerchief,
and I in my cap,
Had just settled our brains
for a long winter's nap;

When out on the lawn
    there arose such a clatter,
I sprang from my bed
    to see what was the matter.
Away to the window
    I flew like a flash,
Tore open the shutters
    and threw up
    the sash.

The moon on the breast
   of the new-fallen snow,
Gave a lustre of mid-day
   to objects below,
When, what to my wondering
   eyes should appear,
But a miniature sleigh,
   and eight tiny rein-deer,
With a little old driver,
   so lively and quick,
I knew in a moment
   it must be St. Nick.

More rapid than eagles
  his coursers they came,
And he whistled, and shouted,
  and called them by name;
"Now, *Dasher*! Now, *Dancer*!
  Now, *Prancer* and *Vixen*!
On, *Comet*! On, *Cupid*!
  On, *Donder* and *Blitzen*!
To the top of the porch!
  to the top of the wall!
Now dash away! dash away!
  dash away all!"

As dry leaves that before
    the wild hurricane fly,
When they meet with an obstacle,
    mount to the sky;
So up to the house-top
    the coursers they flew,
With the sleigh full of Toys,
    and St. Nicholas too.

And then in a twinkling,
I heard on the roof,
The prancing and pawing
of each little hoof—

As I drew in my head,
    and was turning around,
Down the chimney St. Nicholas
    came with a bound.

He was dressed all in fur,
   from his head to his foot,
And his clothes were all tarnished
   with ashes and soot;

A bundle of Toys he had
   flung on his back,
And he looked like a pedlar
   just opening his pack.
His eyes—how they twinkled!
   his dimples, how merry!
His cheeks were like roses,
   his nose like a cherry!

His droll little mouth
    was drawn up like a bow,
And the beard
    of
    his
    chin
    was
    as
    white
    as
    the
    snow;

The stump of a pipe
   he held tight in his teeth,
And the smoke it encircled
   his head like a wreath;
He had a broad face
   and a little round belly,
That shook when he laughed,
   like a bowlfull of jelly.

He was chubby and plump,
 a right jolly old elf,
And I laughed when I saw him,
 in spite of myself,
A wink of his eye
 and a twist of his head,
Soon gave me to know
 I had nothing to dread;

He spoke not
    a word,
    but went
    straight to
    his work,
And fill'd all
    the stockings;
    then turned
    with a jerk,

And laying his finger
   aside of his nose,
And giving a nod,
   up the chimney he rose;

He sprang to his sleigh,
    to his team gave a whistle,
And away they all flew
    like the down of a thistle.

But I heard him exclaim,
ere he drove out of sight,

"HAPPY CHRISTMAS to all . . .
AND TO ALL A GOOD NIGHT."

A NOTE ABOUT THE ILLUSTRATOR
REGINALD BIRCH 1856–1943

REGINALD BIRCH was born in London, England. When he was a teenager, his family traveled around the world. They stopped in San Francisco, California, where Birch met the portrait painter Rosenthal, who encouraged him to pursue art studies. Birch received his first commission in San Francisco: Using oil paints, he camouflaged the black eye of a man who had been in a fight.

In 1873 Birch moved to Europe to study art. He returned to the United States eight years later and made it his home. In 1881 *St. Nicholas Magazine* published an illustration he had created for a poem, thus beginning a career as the creator of thousands of images for magazines and newspapers as well as the illustrator of more than a hundred books. Birch is best known for his illustrations for Francis Hodgson Burnett's classics *Little Lord Fauntleroy* and *The Secret Garden,* and Louisa May Alcott's *Little Men.* His skill, humor, and charm continue to distinguish him as one of the most beloved illustrators in the world.

www.HarcourtBooks.com

LC 2002114878

First gift edition 2003
A C E G H F D B

The display type was set in Wellsbrook Initials.
The text type was set in Garamond.
Color separations by Bright Arts Ltd., Hong Kong
Manufactured by
South China Printing Company, Ltd., China
This book was printed on 100 gsm Munken Print paper.
Production supervision by Sandra Grebenar
and Ginger Boyer